Keeping Quiet

A ZEBRA BOOK

Written by David Lloyd
Illustrated by Malcolm Livingstone

PUBLISHED BY
WALKER BOOKS
LONDON

Ben was asleep on the floor.
There were toys all
round him.
'I'll tidy up,' Polly thought.
'I'll do it very quietly
so I don't wake up Ben.'

Very, very quietly Polly
collected Ben's blocks.
'I'll just make a tower,'
she thought.
'I'll do it very quietly
so I don't wake up Ben.'

Very, very quietly Polly
collected the animals.
'I'll put them by the
tower,' she thought.
'I'll do it very quietly
so I don't wake up Ben.'

Bzzzzzzz!
A clockwork beetle went
buzzing across the floor.

Bzzz

'Shhhh!' Polly said,
catching the beetle.
'You'll wake up Ben.'

z z z z!

Boing!
Jack jumped out of his box.

Boing!

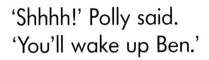

'Shhhh!' Polly said.
'You'll wake up Ben.'

Very, very quietly
Polly moved the drum
and the trumpet.
'It's all so quiet
when Ben's asleep,'
she thought.

Polly sat on the floor.
Everything was tidy.
Ben was still asleep.

'Keeping quiet is difficult,'
she thought.

Polly lay down.
Very, very quietly she
played at sleeping lions.
Soon she fell asleep.

Ben woke up.
Polly was asleep.

Ben toddled
towards the tower.
Polly was asleep.

Ben reached towards the tower.
Polly was asleep.

Crash! The tower fell down.
Bang! Blocks hit the drum.
Boing! Jack jumped out again.
Bzzz! The beetle buzzed away.

Crash!

Polly woke up.

Ben and Polly were both awake.
Bang! Bang! Bang!
Polly played the drum.

Bang!
Bang!
Bang!

Toot! Toot! Toot!
Ben played the trumpet.
'Being noisy is easy,' Polly thought.

Toot!
 Toot!
Toot!